This Book Belongs To

_____

_____

this book is dedicated to
Zoey Duncan

written and illustrated by
Mark D. Pendergrass
with Rhandi Pendergrass

Waylon & Stogie
name/logo
and
Animadelphia
are property of DreamWordZ

special guest appearance by
Zeus the Chameleon
as the orphan boy
owned by **HD Chams**

The Scavenger Hunt
is a work of fiction. Any resemblance
to real people, places, or
events is purely coincidental.

ISBN-13: 978-0692389362
ISBN-10: 0692389369

DreamWordZ
P R O D U C T I O N S

DreamWordZ
presents

WAYLON & STOGIE

in

THE SCAVENGER HUNT

written and illustrated by
Mark D. Pendergrass
with Rhandi Pendergrass

Posters had gone up all over town, and the kids in Animadelphia were gathering to hear about something called a scavenger hunt.

Everyone was excited to hear about what it was and what the winning prize would be... especially Waylon and Stogie.

As they waited for Mayor Pullman to speak, Stogie asked Waylon, "What do you think the big prize will be?"

"I don't know," answered Waylon, "but whatever it is, I'm gonna win it!"

"Oh yeah?" said Stogie. "Well, you're gonna have to work pretty hard to beat me."

At that, Mayor Pullman stood up and began his speech.

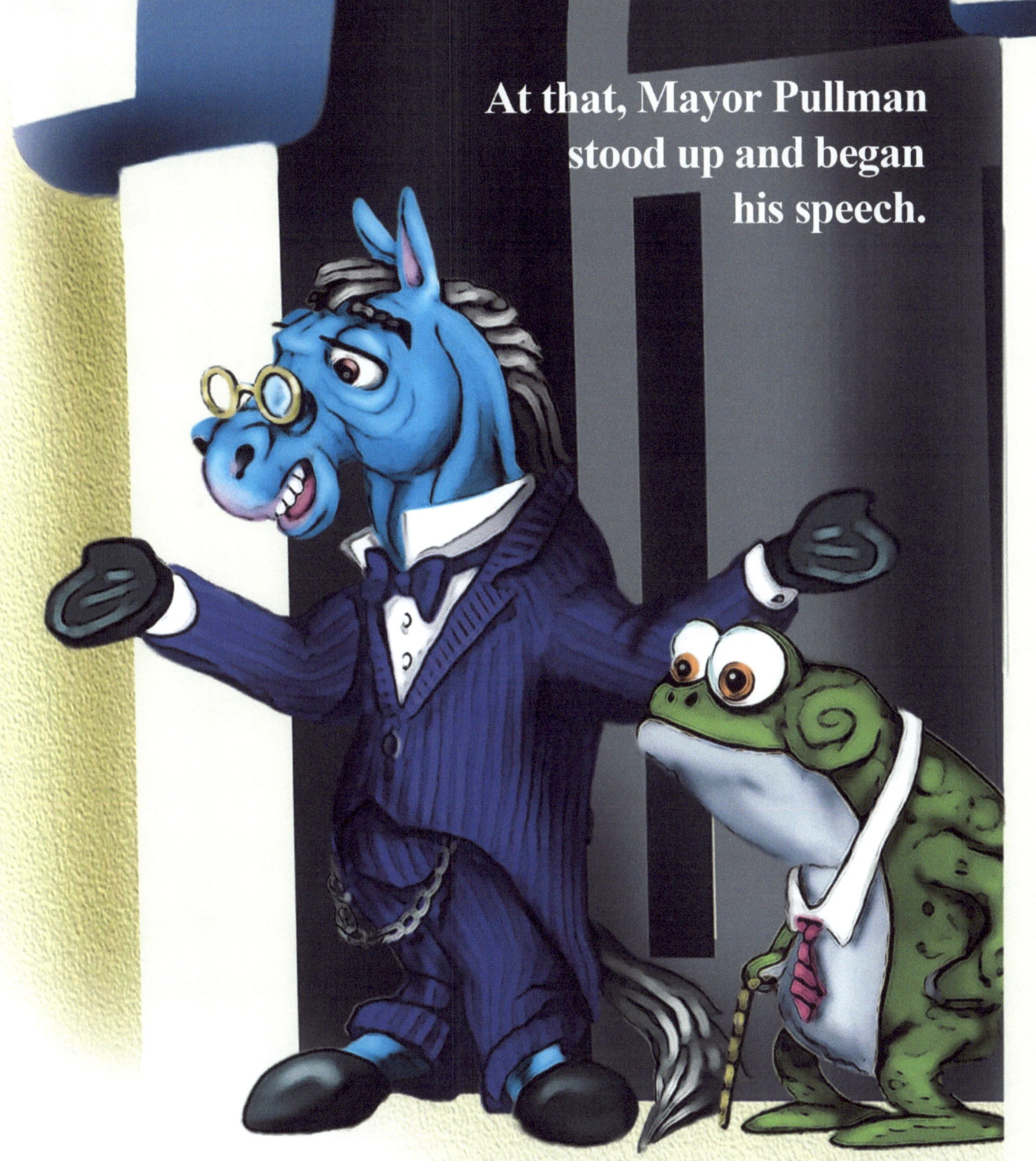

"The First Annual Animadelphia Scavenger Hunt is about to start," he said, "and all the children in Animadelphia will be competing for the GRAND PRIZE."

"Whoever brings in the most items on this list in one hour will be richly rewarded. You must find the items or ask someone to donate them. Everything collected will go to the children at Mother Terrapin's Orphanage."

LIST:

MARBLES
BASEBALL
YO-YO
BUCKET
DOLL
CRAYONS
PUPPET
BOARD GAME
PUZZLE
JAX
MTT
BLOCKS
BAT
TEA SET
GOGGLES
RUBBER DUCK
WHISTLE
RATTLE
BOOK
FLASHLIGHT
FOOTBALL
TOY TRUCK
ROBOT
TOP
RAY GUN
RING TOSS

"Hey, Stogie! Did you hear that?" Waylon exclaimed as his eyes grew even bigger than their usual size. "GRAND PRIZE! RICH REWARD! Now I just *have* to win!"

After getting their lists, Waylon and Stogie heard the starting bell and set off to collect as many items as they could, as *fast* as they could.

Children from one end of Animadelphia to the other were searching high and low, knocking on doors, and asking neighbors for help.

Soon, Purrdy was carrying an
armload of items. Cotton wasn't having as
much luck, but still she was close to catching up.

By the time the hunt was half over, Stogie had an impressive box-full of items. He was running from house to house, stone to stump as fast as his little legs could carry him.

Waylon wasn't doing so well. The clock was
running out and all he had managed
to collect was a tea set
and a bag of marbles.

The grand prize seemed to be slipping from his
grasp and he was beginning to get discouraged.

"I can never win like this," Waylon said to himself. But as he looked more closely at the list, an idea popped into his head.

That's it! he thought. *The rules are... find or DONATE. I have some of these things in my toy box! I can donate my own toys and maybe win the GRAND PRIZE after all.*

With that, he rushed home, his tail wagging with excitement.

As soon as he arrived he began to pile items from the list, one by one, into his wagon.

What a stroke of luck! Waylon thought as he imagined himself standing in front of the whole town to receive his rich reward.

As his wagon became more and more full, and his toy box became more and more empty, Waylon started to wonder if the grand prize was going to be worth it.

Of course it will, he reminded himself.
I'll be RICH!

Quickly, he emptied the last few toys from
his toy box, and began pushing the heavy
wagon up the street toward Town Hall.

Stogie was still knocking on doors when he saw Waylon pass. *I guess Waylon is gonna win the grand prize after all,* he thought.

But the race wasn't over. Purrdy and Cotton, and a whole lot of others were still pushing, pulling, and dragging their piles of scavenged items toward the finish line.

Lucia was almost there but
her little cart was piled so high she was
having trouble keeping things from
falling to the ground.

She and Waylon were neck and neck! Just one more foot and the race would be over.

In one final push, Waylon and Lucia crossed the finish line at the very same time! As others were crossing, the final bell sounded.

Now, only one question remained...
    Who was going to win the grand prize?

Each pile was examined, and each item was
    marked-off on the official scoreboard.

When everything was tallied, Waylon had won by a baseball mitt.

I really love that mitt, Waylon thought, but it was worth losing it to win the GRAND PRIZE!

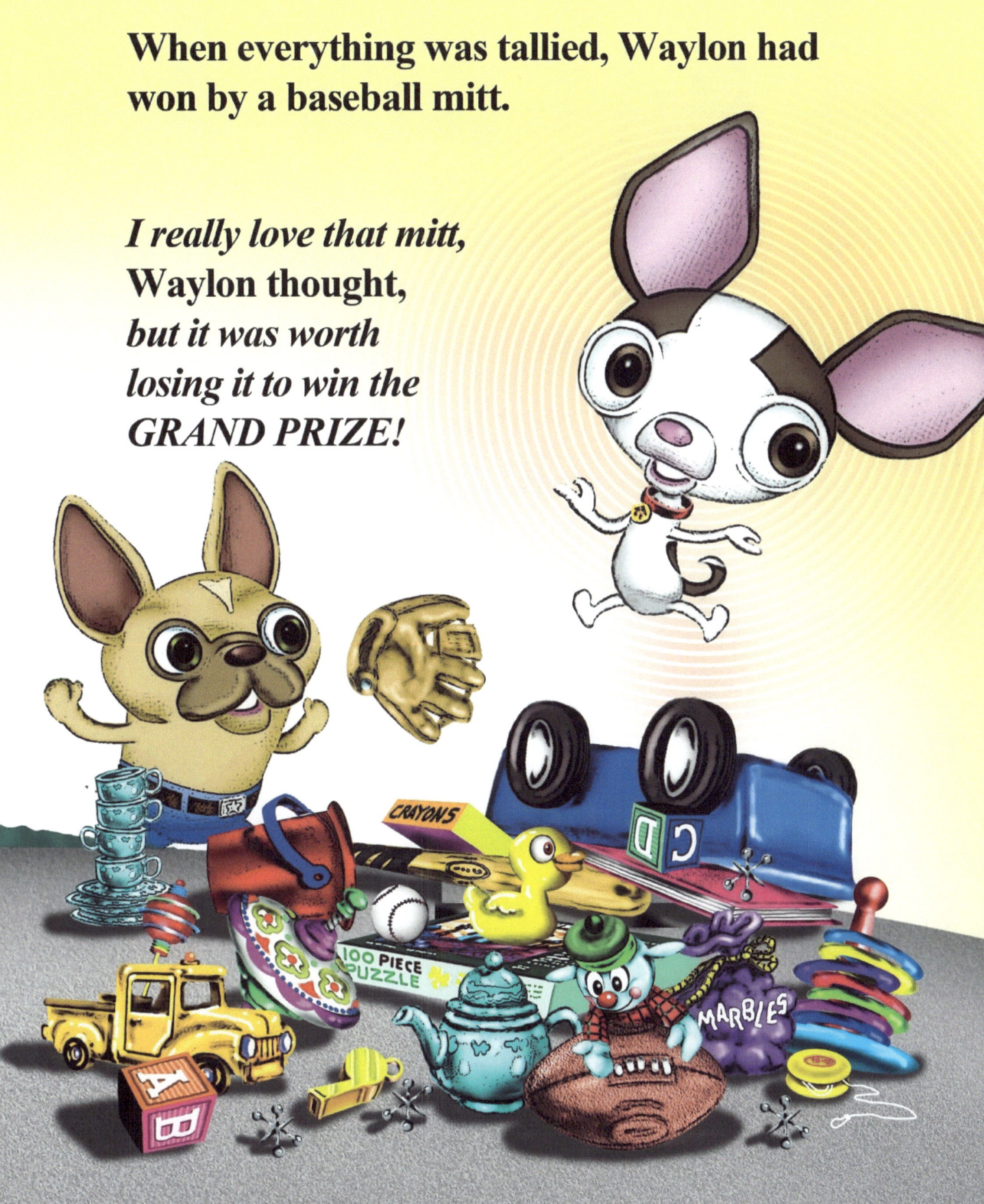

While the other kids added their items to the pile, Waylon could hardly wait to find out what the grand prize would be.

Suddenly, a firm hand touched Waylon's shoulder. It was Mayor Pullman beaming with pride.

"Congratulations young man," he said. "You found all the items on the list and made it back in time to win. Now, for that rich reward you were promised..."

As the Mayor was speaking, Waylon noticed children from the orphanage passing by the mountain of toys. Each one was taking their pick from all the wonderful items that had been collected.

"And what is the GRAND PRIZE, Sir?"
Waylon asked as he jumped
up and down with
excitement.

"You and the children from
the orphange will be pictured on
the front page of the Animadelphia
Gazette, along with all the gifts they
received," brayed the Mayor.
"A RICH REWARD indeed!"

Waylon watched as one of the boys took from the pile, the very mitt that he himself had once treasured.

What a waste! he thought. *I can't believe I traded my mitt for a lousy picture in the paper.*

But as the boy approached him, Waylon could see tears in his eyes.

"Thanks for this awesome gift!"
the boy said. "I've never
had a mitt of my
very own."

Waylon was speechless. To think that
someone had never owned a mitt
seemed very strange to him.

Before Waylon had a chance to finish that
thought, a girl walked up to him
holding the tea set he
had found.

"Thank you for the tea set,"
she said as she gave him a hug.
"I will treasure it forever."

By watching the faces of
the children instead of
watching his toys
disappear...

...Waylon was
beginning to understand how
rewarding it is to make others happy.

MARBLES

Cold dog bites hot dog:
Story and details
on page 13

SPECIAL EDITION

Today's Weather:
Better than yesterday;
worse than tomorrow

THE
5¢ ANIMADELPHIA 5¢
GAZETTE
All the news · an animal needs

SCAVENGER HUNT WINNER

LOCAL BOY RECEIVES RICH REWARD

Along with all those who participated in giving and collecting toys for the orphans (picture courtesy of Mother Terrapin)

KIDS WIN BIG

Yesterday: Town Hall
Mayor Pullman and Town Council Chairman F. A. O. Warts officiated the First Annual Charity Scavenger Hunt for the children of Mother Terrapin's Orphanage.
Lots of toys were collected by local children. A list was given to each child and they were given an hour to collect as many toys as possible.

The grand prize: Being pictured on the front page of the newspaper.
The one to bring in the most items on the list... (See page 4)

DIVING PRO PROVES PROWESS

Animadelphia Falls, a favorite local swimming spot was witness to the spectacular performance of Fitch Twitchel, world famous diver, as he entertained an audience of bears who had come to observe his most recent attempt to dive up the falls.

In a display of both energy and determination, Fitch perfectly executed his trademark "thrust, flip, kick, twist, and wiggle" dive, over and over again, until on the fifteenth try, he made it up the falls and into the waiting arms of his admirers.
A BBQ followed the event, which was an overwhelming success.

Fitch Twitchel shown here with one of his fans. UPI

Correction:
Last Thursday
we reported that the
Women's Knitting Club
was predicting the end
of the world on Saturday.
Actually, they were
predicting the end of
The World Series
on Saturday.
We hope this mistake did
not cause anyone any
inconvenience.
~ Editor ~

THE END

...time to read it over again!

"Giving gifts is more satisfying than receiving them."

email
waylonandstogie@att.net
visit
www.facebook.com/Waylon.Stogie
www.colorspiracy.com

Waylon & Stogie